A Personal Tour of
ELLIS ISLAND

ROBERT YOUNG

⌐ LERNER PUBLICATIONS COMPANY ▪ MINNEAPOLIS

Cover: *Thousands of immigrants passed through the Great Hall on their way to a new life in the United States.*
Title page: *This complex of structures on Ellis Island was designed for the efficient processing of immigrants,*

The author wishes to give special thanks to Barry Moreno, librarian at the Ellis Island Immigration Museum, for patiently answering endless questions, returning numerous phone calls, and providing an outstanding tour of a very special place. Many thanks to the knowledgeable National Park Service rangers at Ellis Island National Monument; to Janet Levine of the Oral History Project and Jeffrey Dosik of the Ellis Island Immigration Museum library for their generous support; to Chris Dall as well as Katy Holmgren for their editorial assistance; and to Sara Young and Tyler Young for their continued interest and encouragement.

For the Powers family of 55 Hermanthau Road— home away from home.

Lerner Publications Company
A division of Lerner Publishing Group
241 First Avenue North
Minneapolis, MN 55401 U.S.A.

Website address: www.lernerbooks.com

LIBRARY OF CONGRESS CATALOGING-IN-PUBLICATION DATA

Young, Robert 1951–
  A personal tour of Ellis Island/by Robert Young
    p. cm.— (How it was)
    Includes index.
    Summary: Describes Ellis Island through the eyes of several people, including a young immigrant and an employee of the Immigration Services, and its various activities and procedures.
    ISBN 0-8225-3579-3 (lib. bdg. : alk. paper)
    1. Ellis Island Immigration Station (N.Y. and N.J.)—Juvenile Literature.
  [1. Ellis Island Immigration Station (N.Y. and N.J.) 2. Emigration and Immigration] I. Title II. Series
  JV6484.Y65   2001
  304.8'73—dc21   99-042054

Manufactured in the United States of America
1 2 3 4 5 6 – JR – 06 05 04 03 02 01

Contents

Ellis Island (above middle) *rises from New York Harbor not far from Manhattan and the Statue of Liberty.*

This was, oh, so amazing when we got . . . into the harbor! . . . When you see Manhattan appear with all these tall buildings . . . it looks as if it's just a lot of tall buildings on a pancake, swimming on water. —Irma Busch

Introduction

Ellis Island Immigration Station sits on a small island in New York Harbor. Between 1892 and 1954, government workers at Ellis Island Immigration Station processed more than 17 million newcomers—most of them from Europe—to the United States. Nearly half of all modern-day U.S. citizens can trace their heritage to a family member who entered the country through Ellis Island. At the immigration center, people who wanted to live in the United States passed through a series of checks and tests. Those who passed were free to enter the country.

Ellis Island wasn't always home to an immigration station. In the 1600s, Native Americans in the area called the island Kioshk (Gull Island) after its only inhabitants. Dutch settlers bought the three-and-a-half acre island in 1630. They renamed it Little Oyster Island because of the delicious oysters found in its sand. The island became part of the British colony of New York in 1664 and changed owners many times over the next century. In 1788 New York itself became the eleventh state of the United States.

At about that time, a New York City merchant named Samuel Ellis owned Little Oyster Island. He built a tavern there, and the island became known as Ellis Island. But the U.S. government wanted to use the site to build a fort in case of war. In 1808 the state of New York bought Ellis Island from the Ellis family. The state sold the island to the U.S. government, which built Fort Gibson on the site. The fort wasn't used during the War of 1812 (1812–1814), but afterward the U.S. Navy stored ammunition there.

Immigration to the United States came in two great waves. The first fell between 1820 and 1880. During this time, most **immigrants** came from western European regions such as Great Britain and what would become Germany. The next period lasted from 1881 until 1930. This period was dominated by immigration from Italy and from eastern European lands, such as Russia. Between 1820 and 1931, almost 6 million German people emigrated, making Germans the largest immigrant group. Italian immigrants formed the second largest group with 4.6 million people.

In the middle of the nineteenth century, immigration to the United States increased. Most newcomers were from Europe, although people from Asia also arrived in large numbers. Some immigrated because earthquakes, famines, and other disasters had affected their lives. Others fled governments that were unfair or harsh. Some left

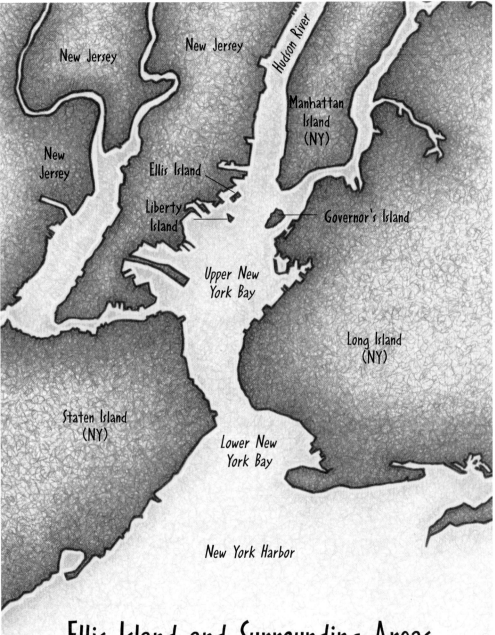

New Jersey

New Jersey

Hudson River

Manhattan
Island
(NY)

New
Jersey

Ellis Island

Liberty
Island

Governor's Island

Upper New
York Bay

Long Island
(NY)

Staten Island
(NY)

Lower New
York Bay

New York Harbor

Ellis Island and Surrounding Areas

After the War of 1812, the U.S. armed forces used Ellis Island to store ammunition.

to escape wars. Many emigrated because they were unable to earn a living. Hearing stories and reading letters from friends and relations who had emigrated, newcomers often thought of the United States as the Land of Opportunity. They hoped to find good jobs, cheap land, and freedom from religious or political persecution and oppression.

Most immigrants from Europe came to the United States on crowded ships that docked in New York City. When the newcomers disembarked, they were often poor and confused. Criminals cheated and robbed many immigrants, some of whom ended up homeless. Some of the new arrivals carried contagious diseases. So New York State's government decided to found an immigrant

Sailing ships carried immigrants to Castle Garden, New York's first immigration station.

station, where newcomers could be carefully and safely processed. An old concert hall called Castle Garden, on the southern tip of Manhattan Island, served as the first processing center. Between 1855 and 1890, eight million immigrants—about seventy percent of all immigrants who arrived in that period—landed at Castle Garden.

As the number of immigrants rose, the U.S. government decided to take charge of immigration. The government looked for a new spot to build a larger, more up-to-date immigration station. They chose Ellis Island. The island site would make it possible to screen, protect, and observe potential immigrants before allowing them to slowly filter into their new culture. Sick people could be **quarantined.** Newcomers would have a place to wait for the friends or family members coming to meet them. The island's site in Upper New York Bay protected it from ocean storms. Manhattan Island, the heart of New York City and the destination of many newcomers, was only a short ferryboat-ride away.

Using landfill (dirt) from Manhattan's subway tunnels and other building sites, workers doubled the size of Ellis Island. They constructed a large depot building for processing the immigrants and built a hospital, a dormitory, and a kitchen.

Ellis Island Immigration Station officially opened on January 1, 1892. During the next five years, 1.5 million immigrants landed at Ellis Island. On June 15, 1897, a fire started in the furnace room and burned the depot to the ground. Luckily, no one was killed.

A new facility, the Main Building, opened its doors in 1901. Four 100-foot-towers flanked a 165-foot-tall, red brick and limestone structure. On the first floor, newcomers could leave their baggage, buy railroad tickets, and rest in a waiting room. On the second floor, the immigrants underwent physical exams and some stayed in detention rooms. Legal exams were held in the Registry Room (also called the Great Hall), a huge room that was one hundred feet wide and two hundred feet long. A kitchen, laundry, and bathhouse were added. Workers used landfill to create a second island connected to the first. A new hospital opened there in 1902, and another hospital opened on a third island in 1911. The linked islands covered a total area of thirty acres. The number of immigrants passing through the station increased from 389,000 a year in 1901 to more than one million in 1907.

The number of immigrants lessened during the First World War (1914–1918). Travel across the Atlantic Ocean became dangerous at this time, and travel across Europe became impossible for many. During this period, the U.S. government used Ellis Island to hold people suspected of supporting the enemy, which included Germany, the **Ottoman Empire,** and the Austro-Hungarian Empire. After the war, the facilities became a place to treat American soldiers who returned with illnesses and wounds. By 1920 processing immigrants was once again the chief activity at Ellis Island, and the number of immigrants increased to about eight hundred thousand a year.

Let's take a closer look at Ellis Island. The year is 1920, and it's a cold morning in February. A steamship is puffing its way up New York Harbor. The ship is filled with immigrants . . . .

The huge Statue of Liberty, a symbol of freedom and tolerance, greeted new arrivals to the United States.

They came with high hopes, so much expectation.
No suitcases, just a bundle of something.

—Irma Busch

With Anna

Anna pushed her way through the crowd of people. She had to get to the railing. All around her, she heard people talking about the statue. Anna wanted see it for herself. Then she would know she was really in the United States. Anna was only ten years old, but she was strong and determined. It wasn't long before she had worked her way across the deck to the rail lining the steamship's deck. She looked across the water and saw the statue right in front of her.

The Statue of Liberty stood tall and straight. The copper figure held her torch high into the air. Excitement buzzed through the crowd. People laughed, shouted, and sang. Some cried with joy.

The cold winter air stung Anna's face, but she didn't mind—the journey was almost over. Anna, her mother, and her two older brothers had traveled a long way from

The Statue of Liberty stands near Ellis Island on Liberty Island in New York's Upper Bay. The statue—a gift to the United States from France—symbolizes freedom and knowledge.

French sculptor Frédéric-Auguste Bartholdi *(above, second from right)* created the famous statue in Europe. In this photo, Bartholdi explains the statue's construction to a visitor while Bartholdi's assistants shape the plaster arm.

Bartholdi and his crew began work in 1871 and finished in 1884. Then they took the statue apart and shipped it to the United States. In 1886 the statue was reassembled on a small island in New York Harbor.

The statue itself is more than 151 feet in height—about fifteen stories. It sits on a sixty-five-foot-tall base with an eighty-nine-foot-tall pedestal. Altogether the monument is 305 feet tall.

their village in Russia to a port on the Baltic Sea. There
they had boarded this steamship. After three long weeks
on the rocking boat, Anna could hardly wait to stand on
solid land again. But Anna was more impatient to see her
father, who already had been in New York City for two
years. He would take them to their new home in an
apartment near the clothing factory where he worked.

Anna was still standing at the railing when the ship
docked. She gazed at the hundreds of strange, tall buildings across the harbor. New York City looked so different

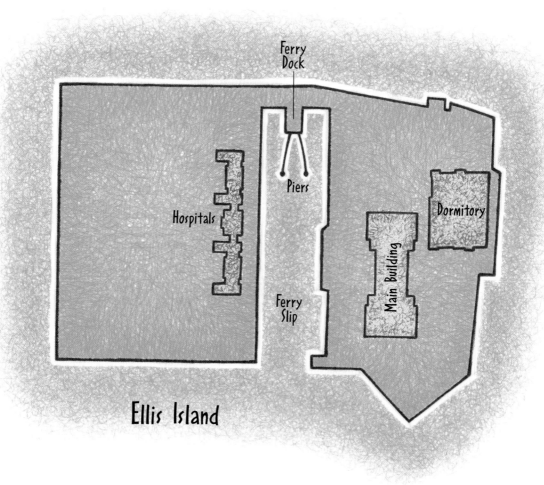

Ferry
Dock

Piers

Hospitals

Dormitory

Main Building

Ferry
Slip

Ellis Island

from any place she had ever seen before. As the crowd around her shifted, Anna gripped her bundle of clothes and her favorite doll. She worried that her only possessions would be knocked out of her arms. The eager crowd pressed forward down a wooden plank to stand on a pier along the Hudson River. Passengers who had traveled by first or second class disembarked here. But Anna knew that she and her family would have to pass through Ellis Island Immigration Station before they could go into New

Ferryboats carried groups of immigrants into the island's slips (openings between docks), where the boats waited in line to unload their passengers.

Before the 1870s, when sailing ships carried immigrants to the United States, the ship's steering equipment was located on the lowest level. The area was called "steerage." When new technology allowed ship-builders to place steering systems in other parts of the ship, the area was used to house third-class, or steerage, passengers. Steerage was the cheapest way to travel, so most immigrants traveled that way.

The ceiling was often only five feet from the floor. Bunk beds or hammocks lined the area. Many passengers had only their bunks to sit on, sleep on, and store their possessions on. An entire steerage might have only one water tap and few bathrooms. Most people got very sea-sick from the rocking of the ship. To make matters worse, no portholes (windows) and poor ventilation kept steerage stuffy and smelly. Shipping companies provided poor food to steerage passengers.

First-class and second-class passengers had private cabins and ate fine meals in elegant dining rooms. When ships came into New York Harbor, immigration workers boarded the ships to examine these passengers, who were quickly cleared to enter the country. Only steerage passengers went to Ellis Island.

York City. Like most of the ship's passengers, Anna and her family had traveled in the steerage compartment. Everyone who traveled steerage had to pass through Ellis Island.

Anna followed her mother and brothers off the ship. It felt strange to stand on land after so long on the rocking boat. Uniformed men shouted in English at the disembarking crowd. Anna didn't understand what they said. Immigration workers organized the mass of people into groups of thirty. Then the workers called out names. When her name was called, a worker pinned a small,

The bags brought by immigrants told stories of their own. Some baggage workers claimed that they could recognize the country that the immigrant was from by the type of luggage they carried and by the way that they tied knots on the ropes around them.

square identification card covered with words and numbers onto her lapel. Anna wished that she could read English. With the cards in place, Anna, her family, and many others walked onto a waiting ferryboat.

The ferryboat soon steamed across the harbor. In a short time, the ferryboat reached a small island in the harbor—Ellis Island. The boat pulled into a slip. Other ferryboats seemed to line the docks. Although the passengers were eager to step onto the island, they had to wait until it was their ferry's turn to unload.

Anna stared at the red and white building stretching in front of her. A tall, copper-domed tower at each of the four corners made it look like a palace. Three arched windows lined the front, and two gables poked from the front of the sloping roof. Two lower wings extended from each side of the main section of the building.

These Belgian refugees arrived on Ellis Island in 1917. In this photo, they are disembarking from a ferryboat and heading for the Main Building.

Some immigrants kept their luggage with them.

Anna remembered her father's letter about his experience at Ellis Island. This was where she would learn whether she could stay in America. But she wasn't too worried—she was healthy and there was a home waiting for her.

Anna pulled her scarf tightly around her head as the wind whipped around her. She wished her father was with them already. The men directed the people from Anna's ferry onto the island. One of the men stayed with Anna's group of thirty people. Anna hugged her bundle as the line slowly moved off the boat and along the dock. The line curved under a long iron roof over a sidewalk, which led to the doorway of the building. Slowly the line passed up the stairs, through the arched doorway, and into a ground-floor room.

Sunlight poured through the windows of the medium-sized room. The noise was deafening. Anna stared in amazement at all of the people crowding into the room. All around her, she heard the sounds of many different languages. People shouted and babies cried. Anna grabbed at her brothers' jackets and pulled them close to her mother. What would happen if one of her brothers got lost? How would he ever be found?

Some of the people left their bundles and baggage in this room. Immigration workers passed out tags to people so that they could pick up their belongings later. But Anna's mother told her to keep her bundle to make sure that it didn't get lost or stolen. The family joined the line of people that snaked across the room and up a wide, steep stairway. Finally Anna and her family reached the steps. Anna looked up to the top of the stairway where she saw a uniformed man who stood at the top of the staircase. His eyes moved over each person trooping past. Anna noticed that he used a piece of chalk to mark some people's shoulders as they passed him at the top of the steps. Anna wondered what the marks meant. She pulled closer to her mother as her brothers slowly led the way up the stairs.

Inspection cards, like this one from 1920, helped immigrants stay with their assigned **manifest** groups and get processed in an orderly way.

One of [the] young men was the leader of a bunch of immigrants. He would . . . say, "Watch me." You watched him, you followed him. . . .

—Theodore Lubik

With Thomas Hill

Thomas Hill glanced at the line of immigrants climbing the stairs. He worked for the Immigration Service as a grouper, which meant that he guided groups of immigrants through the inspection process. The group was made up of the thirty people on one manifest. On this day, Thomas was responsible for Irish immigrants. He had to make sure that they stayed together and got examined at Ellis Island. Thomas was glad that he could talk to them without using an interpreter, and he found their accents easy to understand. Thomas had been born in the United States, but his parents had come from Ireland many years before. They had even come through Ellis Island.

Although a few people in Thomas's group were children, most were adults. They looked serious as they walked up the stairs. With each step, they inched closer to the exams that would determine who could stay in America. First there would be the medical exam. Intelligence tests for the immigrants whom doctors suspected had mental problems would follow. Finally, an inspector would give the immigrants legal exams. People who failed these tests could be sent back to their home country.

Although the immigrants didn't know it, the medical exam had already begun. A doctor from the Public Health Service stood at the top of the stairs, watching the immigrants as they walked toward him. If he saw a person limping or out of breath, the doctor made a chalk mark on the person's coat to indicate the problem. Many people didn't notice that happen. Thomas noticed a few members of his group had marks on their shoulders.

When all the people from Thomas's group reached the top of the stairs, Thomas led them to lines where they could be examined by doctors. Males and females stood in separate lines. Some of the immigrants had chalk marks on their backs.

In the medical exam area, more doctors checked the immigrants. Although the exam took only a few minutes, the doctors checked for more than

Steamship companies recorded names and other information about passengers on lists called manifests. Each manifest page had a letter code, and each passenger was assigned a number. Each page listed about thirty people. Ship captains provided the lists to Ellis Island inspectors, who made copies of the manifests. Before entering Ellis Island, workers gave each ship passenger a card with a manifest page code and a special number. The cards provided information that made it easier for officials to use the manifests to process the immigrants.

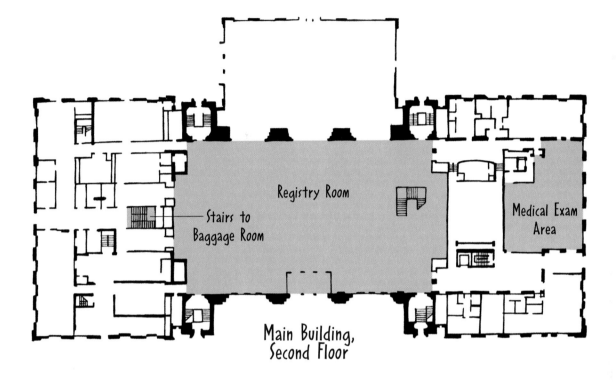

Registry Room

Stairs to
Baggage Room

Medical Exam
Area

Main Building,
Second Floor

fifty different problems. First came a painful eye exam. The doctors used buttonhooks (small metal devices designed to button gloves and shoes) to roll back each person's eyelids. The doctors were looking for signs of trachoma, a contagious disease that caused blindness and death. No one with trachoma could enter the United States. In between patients, each doctor dipped his buttonhook in a bowl of alcohol to disinfect it. Each wiped his hands on a dirty-looking towel hanging nearby.

Thomas watched the immigrants grimace during the eye exam. Others shifted uncomfortably as they waited their turns. A few children whimpered and climbed into their parents' arms. After the eye exam, Thomas directed

The U.S. government wanted to make sure that only healthy people entered the country. The doctors at Ellis Island checked immigrants for signs of contagious diseases that could cause harm to others. They also looked for serious physical problems that could prevent an immigrant from earning a living.

When Public Health Service doctors suspected that an immigrant had medical problems, the doctors marked that immigrant's shoulder or back using a piece of chalk. The mark was easy to see on the dark clothes most people wore and could be dusted away later.

Some of the chalk markings were codes. If an immigrant seemed to have a back problem, for example, the doctor would mark a B. Other codes included L for lameness, F for face, Ft for feet, G for **goiter**, H for heart, Pg for pregnancy, Sc for scalp, and X for mental problems. In other cases, the doctors wrote the entire word to signal other possible medical problems. They wrote out *measles, nails, skin, vision,* and *voice.*

each person to the next line of doctors. He told a few people to unbutton their high collars so that the doctors could check for goiters (large, swollen glands) and tumors. Anyone with a hat or kerchief was asked to remove it. The doctors would look for **favus,** which was a contagious skin disease caused by a fungus.

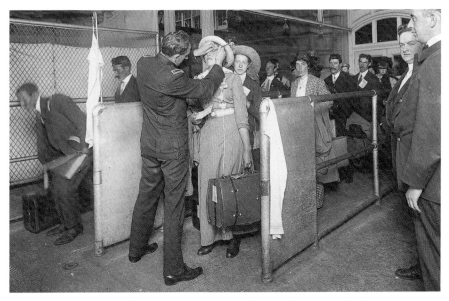

Doctors checked each immigrant's eyes for a disease called trachoma.

To rule out posture and gait problems, the doctors made immigrants put down their boxes and bundles. The examiners then watched the people walk. To check for deafness, doctors asked children to reply to questions. And the doctors asked questions of immigrants who weren't attentive or who didn't appear smart.

Almost all of Thomas's group passed the tests. Thomas gathered the few who had chalk marks. He led a few men down a hallway to small rooms where they sat to wait for another, more thorough medical exam. A matron accompanied some women to similar rooms. If the exam revealed any disease, the immigrant would head to one of the hospitals on Ellis Island. There he or she could recover before entering the United States. Some people with then incurable diseases would be returned to their home country.

Groups waited on the benches in the Registry Room.

Thomas led the rest of his group—the ones who had not been marked with chalk—into the Registry Room, where they would take a legal exam. Although the room seemed packed, Thomas found a few benches for his group to rest on. Thomas could tell from the crowd that it would be a long wait.

Thomas smiled as he watched the immigrants look around in awe. Light flooded enormous arched windows and glared off the high, tiled ceiling. From the ceiling hung metal and glass chandeliers. Thomas gazed at the American flag extending from the long balcony overlooking the room. He knew that the flag was a symbol of hope

The U.S. flag hangs high in the Great Hall.

for the immigrants all around him. He thought of his own parents, who had passed through Ellis Island years before and who had found a happy life in the United States.

In 1916, during World War I, German spies set fire to U.S. ammunition barges in New York Harbor. When the barges exploded, the original plaster ceiling of the Registry Room was badly damaged. The ceiling was replaced in 1917 by Rafael Guastavino, an immigrant who had come to America from Spain in 1881. He chose to use terra-cotta tiles because they were light, strong, fireproof, and inexpensive. Guastavino used more than twenty-eight thousand tiles to finish the ceiling. Rather than using scaffolding, Guastavino's workmen strapped themselves into safety belts. They did their work dangling from the ceiling!

This legal inspector carefully checks an immigrant's documents against a manifest.

I remember officers, officials with blue coats and brass buttons going back and forth. —Thomas Rogan

With Inspector Simpson

At the west end of the Registry Room, Inspector George Simpson shifted his position on a tall, wooden stool. He tapped the edges of a stack of landing cards that he would give to the immigrants who passed his inspection, and then set the stack at the edge of his small, wooden desk. On the desk lay copies of ships' manifests. George turned the page of a registry ledger, where he recorded his decision on each immigrant who came before him. Like the other inspectors, he had to decide if an immigrant was, in the words of the law, "clearly and beyond a doubt entitled to land." He worked to make the correct choice.

George glanced along the row of fifteen to twenty legal inspectors working in the Registry Room. Then he lifted his eyes to see the hundreds of people who filled the Registry Room. Most immigrants sat on a series of long wooden benches stretching the length of the room, but

31

others stood or paced. George dipped his fountain pen in a bottle of ink, then called out a manifest number.

A grouper guided immigrants toward George's desk. The group huddled together, and George noticed that they looked tired and nervous. He called an older woman forward. A long, brown coat covered her faded gray dress, and a plaid kerchief neatly covered her white hair. She clutched a straw basket covered with a cloth. George saw fear in the woman's eyes as she stepped up to the desk.

George glanced at the identification tag pinned to the woman's coat. He used the numbers on the tag to find the page and line in the manifest where this woman's name appeared. Next to her name he saw the answers to thirty-two questions that a representative from the shipping company had asked the woman before her voyage. George would repeat each question she'd been asked. If she replied differently, it could mean the woman wasn't being truthful, which could keep her from passing the legal exam.

The woman, who was from Hungary,

Legal inspectors asked each adult immigrant the same questions. They asked for an immigrant's full name, age, sex, marital status, occupation, nationality, last residence, point of departure, and destination. They asked who had paid for the passage, how much money the immigrant had, if he or she had a criminal record, whether he or she had relatives in the United States, and if he or she had a job waiting in the United States.

Legal inspectors allowed only children accompanied by an adult to gain entry. Women had to have a man with them or waiting for them. Immigrants with jobs waiting for them weren't admitted, but neither were people who might not be able to work.

didn't speak English. This wasn't a problem because each inspector worked with an interpreter. Many interpreters at Ellis Island knew six to twelve different languages. George asked the woman questions through an interpreter, who relayed her replies to George. The answers matched the information recorded on the manifest, so George asked to see her money.

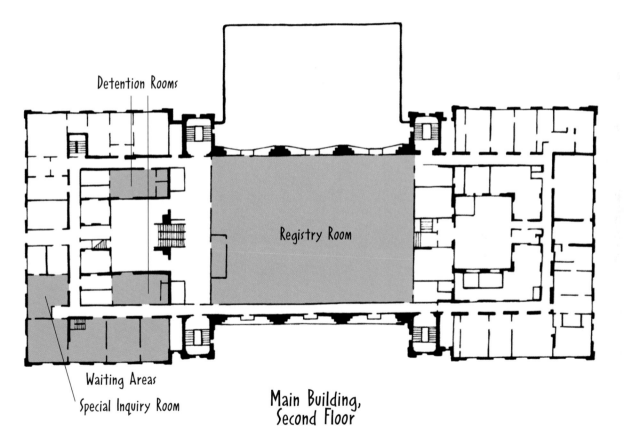

Detention Rooms

Registry Room

Waiting Areas

Special Inquiry Room

Main Building,
Second Floor

In the early years of Ellis Island, immigrants waiting for legal inspections stood for hours in rows separated by metal railings. The bars kept people in orderly lines. Between 1905 and 1909, workers removed the railings and installed wooden benches so that immigrants could sit down during their long wait.

Regulations suggested that, to enter the United States, people needed some money to make sure they wouldn't become beggars. The Hungarian woman had enough. George asked her to read aloud a short passage in her native language. The translator assured George that the woman was able to read. Then the woman passed the translator a crumpled telegram, which read that her family members already in the United States would sponsor her and meet her at Ellis Island. George handed her a landing card and wrote her name into his register. The woman was free to enter the United States.

The next immigrant, a man, gave answers that didn't match those on the list. He had no money, and George doubted that this man had the skills to get a job. He used chalk to mark an SI (Special Inquiry) on the man's sleeve, then sent the immigrant over to the waiting room of the board of Special Inquiry. The man would have to be questioned further.

George rubbed his eyes, which were tired from reading the small writing on the manifests. He changed his focus to gaze at the huge arched window in the eastern wall. Then he glanced at the people standing on the balcony that lined the upper part of the room. Some Immigration

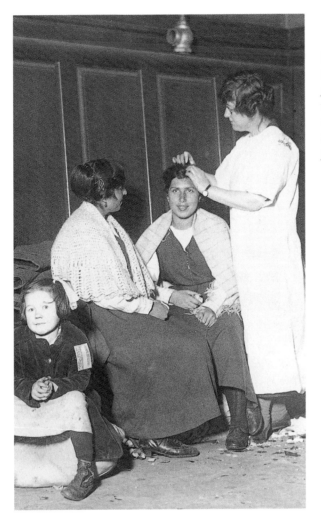

Female inspectors, called matrons, conducted physical examinations of women. They inspected the immigrants for lice, as shown in this 1921 photograph.

Service workers looked down at the crowd. George spotted a few immigrants from the third-floor dormitories. They stood side-by-side with government officials, watching the immigration processing firsthand.

Inspector Simpson pulled at his starched collar and straightened his wool jacket. He had a hard, tiring job. He

About twenty out of every one hundred immigrants were made to come before the board of Special Inquiry. Only about two of the twenty were deported, or sent back to their native countries.

worked from nine o'clock in the morning until seven o'clock at night, seven days a week. During those hours, he questioned hundreds of immigrants and, in the few minutes he was with them, made a judgment that would shape their lives. Though it was a hard job, George Simpson felt proud to be an inspector at Ellis Island. He knew most of the people he admitted would live better lives here than they would have in their home countries.

In 1885 the U.S. Congress passed a law stating that employers couldn't make contracts with immigrants to bring them to the United States and provide them with jobs. Congress believed that the immigrants would accept lower wages than American workers. This could encourage employers not to hire people already living in the country. So immigrants had to show that they were able to work, but that they didn't already have a job.

Around the time of World War I, many Americans became concerned about the number of immigrants coming to the United States. The Americans felt that the immigrants' religious and ethnic backgrounds would make it hard for them to mix into U.S. culture. They worried that uneducated newcomers would be a drain on American resources. So Congress passed laws that changed the rules for immigration. Starting in 1917, all immigrants over the age of sixteen had to prove they could read by taking a literacy test in their native language.

People wait for their turn facing the board of Special Inquiry. These men hope to be allowed to remain in the United States.

*One by one they were calling us into the office
and asking us questions.*

—Vera Gauditsa

With Joseph

Joseph sat in his father's office in the Great Hall's east wing. He stared at the stack of files on the wooden table in front of him. He'd spent a long morning alphabetizing the files. Ready to do something different, he squirmed in his seat. He liked spending his school holiday at his father's office, but he felt that he'd been sitting long enough.

Early that morning, Joseph and his father had taken the ferry from Manhattan to Ellis Island. An Immigration Service employee in the Record Division, Joseph's father kept track of the detention records, lists of immigrants who had been **detained** for medical or legal reasons. He also organized manifests and the cards inspectors had filled out for each immigrant who came to Ellis Island. His job was to make sure that the records were complete and well organized.

39

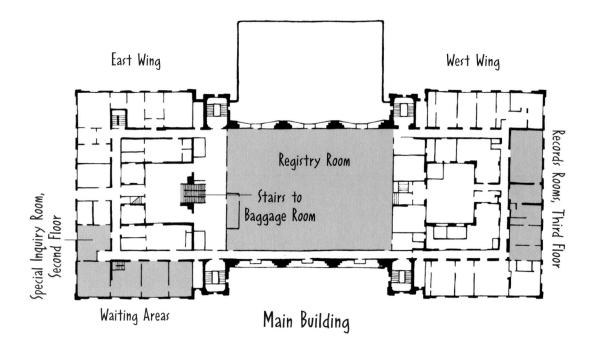

Finally, Joseph's father let the boy head to the Registry Room. Joseph's grandparents had emigrated from Italy and had taught Italian to Joseph. At age twelve, Joseph was so fluent that he was always welcomed by the busy workers at the Immigration Station. He helped by interpreting for Italian immigrants at Ellis Island.

Joseph raced out of the office, down the narrow hall, and up a flight of stairs to the second floor. He walked into the Registry Room and stood at the eastern end. He saw the unending line of people trudging up the stairs from the Baggage Room and heard the muffled sound of voices and feet.

As he moved along the edge of the Registry Room, Joseph saw bearded men wearing heavy wool jackets and women dressed in aprons and colorful kerchiefs. People carried boxes, baskets, and battered suitcases. Voices spoke in many different languages. He heard laughter, babies crying, the gruff voices of parents disciplining their children, and the sound of shuffling feet.

Joseph wove expertly through the crowd. He watched people take their turns standing before the legal inspector. Those who passed the inspection walked down the stairs at the end of the room. Workers led the people who had failed the inspection through a door on the southern side of the room, where Joseph headed. He followed an Immigration Service worker leading a woman and her two small children out the doorway. The woman had SI marked on her shoulder. Joseph heard the man speaking in English. Joseph could tell from her protests in Italian that she did not understand the man.

Joseph followed them through the door, down the hall, and into a small waiting room with a white tile floor and tall, thin windows. Several immigrants sat in wooden chairs and whispered to each other in languages Joseph recognized as Hungarian, Swedish, and German. He didn't understand what they said, but he hoped that someday he would know many languages.

Joseph spoke in English with a worker sitting behind a desk, and then the boy turned to the woman and explained in Italian that she hadn't been approved to enter the United States. She didn't have enough money to provide for herself and her children. The woman told Joseph she had relatives living in the United States who would help her. They would meet her here at Ellis Island. Joseph told her not to worry. Everything would probably be all right after she faced a board of Special Inquiry.

He told her that five different boards, each made up of three inspectors, met in the Great Hall every day. Each board worked to decide the cases of detained immigrants. In this case, a board would decide if the woman could prove that her American relatives were willing and able to help her. The decision would be based on a majority vote of the board's three inspectors. Soon an Immigration Service worker opened a wooden door with a window of smoked glass. He called the woman and her children into the Special Inquiry room.

The worker held the door open for the family. Joseph wished the mother luck. Because her relatives were meeting her, it would be easy to show that they intended to help her. He started to follow her into the Special Inquiry room. The shiny wooden floor looked clean. A high ceiling and large windows that let in plenty of light made the room feel larger than it was. Silver radiators on the outside walls helped keep the room warm. At the far end of the room stood a long wooden desk. Joseph saw the three inspectors sitting behind the desk and waiting to hear cases.

A few feet of space separated the desk from polished wood railings and an aisle. Behind the railings, the woman sat on a bench with her children next to her. When it was time to be questioned by the board, she would walk between the railings and up to the desk. Standing nearby would be an official interpreter. Joseph knew that the woman would be able to tell her story to

The board of Special Inquiry made life-changing decisions in the SI rooms, like the one above. The rooms resembled small courtrooms with several desks for the SI inspectors to use for taking notes.

the board without his help, so he ducked back into the waiting room and turned left into the hallway. Walking along the west wing, Joseph passed waiting rooms and Special Inquiry rooms. He hurried past offices for the Deporting Division, the group charged with sending back excluded immigrants. He spotted a few rooms used to hold excluded immigrants until they could be deported. Some would be on the same ships on which they had traveled to the United States.

When Joseph reached the north side of the building, he found the stairs that led to the third floor. He walked along the balcony overlooking the Registry Room. To his

Detained people rested on hard metal bunks in dormitories.

left lay the men's dormitories. The dorms for women sat on the other side of the balcony.

Joseph stepped into one of the men's dormitory rooms and looked around. A metal lamp hung from the center of the high ceiling. The clean, white walls showed plaster on the bottom half and tiles on the top half. Several boys and men talked quietly on the metal bunk beds lining the room.

Joseph could sense the sadness in the room. The men and boys in the dormitories were being detained at Ellis Island. Some were just waiting for their paperwork. Others needed more money or the promise of someone to be responsible for them before they could legally enter the

United States. Officials suspected others of being wanted criminals or of having run away from their families. The board of Special Inquiry had determined that these men weren't fit to enter the United States. Although some would probably appeal the decision, many of the men would surely be sent back to their homelands.

Back out on the balcony, Joseph leaned on the wooden railing. He gazed down at the Registry Room. He watched immigrants with landing cards move toward the stairs at the western end of the room. Joseph knew that these lucky people were on their way to new lives in America. He wondered what would happen to people who couldn't enter. What would their lives be like back in Europe?

Observers watch the newcomers in the Great Hall. Most immigrants would become residents of the United States.

To buy railroad tickets, immigrants exchanged their money for U.S. currency.

When I left Ellis Island, it was one happy day. —Ida Mouradjian

With Heidi

Heidi wept quietly as Franz, her husband, gathered their small family together at the west end of the Registry Room. When they had left their home in Germany, Heidi had cried from sorrow and from fear because she hadn't known what would happen to them. Heidi's tears at Ellis Island were tears of joy. Her family had just received their landing cards. They could stay in America!

A tall Ellis Island employee wearing a blue uniform shouted to Heidi, Franz, their two children, and the others standing at the end of the hall. He and several other workers organized the immigrants into groups with the same destination. Heidi and her family joined the group headed for Scranton, Pennsylvania, because they were going to stay with Franz's brother in that town.

The uniformed men led the groups down the stairs to

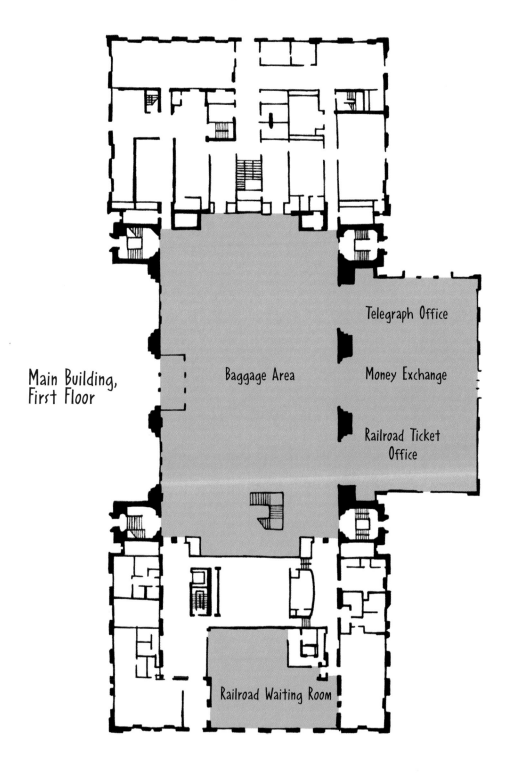

Main Building,
First Floor

Telegraph Office

Money Exchange

Railroad Ticket
Office

Baggage Area

Railroad Waiting Room

the first floor of the building. At the bottom of the stairs, friends and family already living in New York City awaited new arrivals. A twenty-minute ferry ride would take them back to Battery Park, at the south end of Manhattan.

Heidi and her family paused at the bottom of the stairs. There was so much confusion! People walked in all different directions. They were laughing, singing, and shouting questions in many different languages. Heidi shivered with excitement.

Franz spotted the telegraph office on the first floor of the Main Building. He wanted to send his brother a telegram to let him know they would soon arrive in Scranton. He could have sent a postcard at the nearby postal counter, but Franz didn't want his brother to wait for the good news. A telegram would arrive much more quickly. But first he would need American money.

Franz and Heidi took the children to the money exchange. Six men stood at counters in wire-enclosed booths. Immigrants waited in lines on the shiny red-tiled floor. As they stood in line, Heidi read the writing on a blackboard hanging from the wall. On it was displayed the rate of exchange, or how many U.S. dollars were equal to money from other countries. Heidi carefully did the math to see how much they would have. She hoped it would be enough to get started as well as to buy a house.

In a short time, Franz, Heidi, and the children reached the front of the line. Heidi handed the **marks** to the man in the booth, who quickly counted them. He wrote some numbers on a paper and pushed some American dollars across the counter to her. Heidi picked up the pile of bills.

She counted them carefully before she stuffed them into her jacket pocket. She had gotten the right amount of money.

Franz had the telegram sent to his brother, then met Heidi and the children in the hallway. They walked the short distance to the baggage room, got their bags, and lugged them over to the railroad ticket office in the back of the building. The large open area, behind the baggage room, was busy with people buying railroad tickets. Booths from many different railroad companies lined the room. Immigrants could buy railroad tickets for destinations across the United States.

On busy days at Ellis Island, railroad clerks as a group often sold twenty-five tickets a minute. They sold tickets to immigrants who had gained access to the United States and would take ferries to various railroad stations in New York and New Jersey. Then the newcomers would depart for destinations across the United States.

Heidi stood with her family in the center of the ticket office and anxiously looked for the group going to Scranton. In all the confusion of sending the telegram and exchanging money, they had lost track of their group and its leader. From which booth should she buy their tickets? How was she supposed to know?

Then she heard a man speaking German in a loud, clear voice. He was answering questions for people. Franz walked over to the man and learned that he worked for an immigrant aid society, a group that helped immigrants. The man was helping German immigrants by answering their questions and directing them to various services. The man pointed out to Franz a railroad booth. Once more the family waited in line. To Heidi it seemed as though that's all they'd done at Ellis Island—wait in lines. Her feet ached, and she longed for the long trip to be

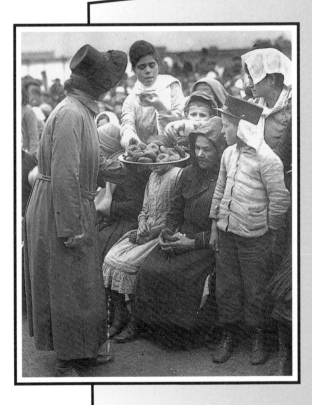

Many groups, such as the Red Cross, YMCA, and Salvation Army, helped immigrants. At Ellis Island, representatives of the groups provided many services for the immigrants. They assisted the newcomers in making appeals to the board of Special Inquiry if they were detained. They passed out food for the hungry travelers and clothing to those who needed it. They also helped the immigrants locate their relatives. Sometimes the aid society members even helped people find work and housing.

An Ellis Island official tags this family in preparation for their railroad trip to the U.S. mainland.

over. After Franz bought the tickets, a worker from the Pennsylvania Railroad pinned a tag on each person's coat. The tags indicated which train the family was taking.

To reach their railroad station, they would take a ferry ride to nearby New Jersey. While they waited for the ferry, Heidi spent some money at a concession stand. She bought a loaf of bread, some sausage, and a few apples. The fresh fruit tasted delicious after all the boiled potatoes, stringy beef, and lukewarm soup they had eaten on the ship. She saved the rest of the food for the train ride.

After what felt like a long time, Heidi's family and the others headed for Scranton followed an Immigration Service worker. As she walked to the ferry, Heidi glanced at the big gray dormitory to her left. She could see the faces of people being held on Ellis Island. Heidi was glad she and her family were free to go.

Franz and the children stepped onto the ferry. At the edge of the dock, Heidi stopped and turned around to look at the Main Building behind her. She would never forget this place or this day. It was her first day in America.

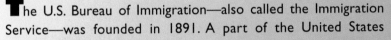

The U.S. Bureau of Immigration—also called the Immigration Service—was founded in 1891. A part of the United States Treasury Department, the organization was in charge of controlling immigration.

In 1937 President Franklin D. Roosevelt combined the Immigration Service with the Naturalization Service, which had been in charge of setting standards for citizenship. The new organization was called the Immigration and Naturalization Service (INS). This agency continues to control immigration in modern times.

This Ellis Island employee waves good-bye to the Immigration Station upon its closing in 1954.

New York Harbor . . . was the most beautiful
sight in the world . . . . We made it. We were
in America . . . . —Regina Rogatta

Afterword

Immigrants continued to be processed at Ellis Island after 1920. But a growing number of people in the United States felt that too many immigrants entered the country. They believed that many of the newcomers were diseased, criminals, and out to take Americans' jobs. As a result, in 1921 President Warren G. Harding signed the Immigration Quota Law, which set monthly limits for immigration. The act linked new immigration to the percentage of each nationality's portion of the U.S. population in 1910. Not more than 3 percent of that population could be admitted to the United States each month. Ships raced to deliver people on the first day of the month. Even so, the number of immigrants arriving at Ellis Island decreased.

In 1924 the National Origins Act made further limits by cutting the number of immigrants to 2 percent of each

After its closing, Ellis Island's buildings deteriorated, even after the island became part of the Statue of Liberty National Monument.

nationality's portion of the U.S. population in 1890. The law declared that immigrants could be inspected in their country of origin, which allowed people to qualify for entry into the United States before making a long ocean voyage.

With the inspections being held overseas, Ellis Island was no longer used as a processing center. The U.S. government instead used Ellis Island to hold foreign-born people who were criminals or viewed as political threats to the country. The U.S. Coast Guard later used it as a training facility. But the buildings were expensive to maintain, so on November 19, 1954, Ellis Island closed.

The buildings on Ellis Island stood vacant for about twenty years. During that time, vandals broke windows and looters took anything they could carry. Roofs collapsed. Plaster and tiles fell from the ceilings. Paint peeled off the walls.

Although the buildings at Ellis Island deteriorated, people remembered them. For many immigrants who had passed through Ellis Island, the immigration station was a symbol of freedom and opportunity. They considered it an important historic site. Many native-born Americans agreed.

Restoration began on Ellis Island's Main Building (above left) *in 1982. The Statue of Liberty* (inset) *was restored around the same time as Ellis Island.*

In 1965 President Lyndon B. Johnson made Ellis Island part of the nearby Statue of Liberty National Monument. The National Park Service administered both sites. Planners hoped to make Ellis Island into a museum devoted to immigration, but a lack of funding prevented construction. In 1970 the National Park Service granted a group permission to develop the island, but denied the permission in 1973 because of the group's financial problems.

In 1974 organizations lobbied Congress for money that would allow the National Park Service to repair Ellis Island's buildings so that tourists could view the historic place. The efforts paid off.

The National Park Service began work on the damaged

This recent visitor to the Ellis Island Immigration Museum is standing by a 1905 photograph that shows his father (front row, far right). *The scene is of young Russian men at the funeral of a friend killed during the Kishinev pogroms (massacres).*

Visitors to the Ellis Island Immigration Museum can view pictures and read stories of immigrants.

sites in 1976. The service began to conduct tours of the Main Building that same year. More than fifty thousand people came to see the famous building.

In 1982 citizens formed the Statue of Liberty/Ellis Island Foundation in order to fund the restoration of both monuments. Many corporations and more than twenty million people contributed money to the effort.

Restoring Ellis Island's Main Building required more work than any other building in U.S. history. New copper domes on the towers, reproductions of period light fixtures, paint that matched the original colors, and new wooden flooring helped re-create the structure's original look. Modern touches, such as a skylight and a glass-and-steel sheltered entrance path, bring the Main Building

Near Ellis Island's Main Building, visitors can search a monument for the names of ancestors who came through Ellis Island.

up to date. The project took eight years to complete and cost $156 million.

On September 10, 1990, the fully restored Ellis Island Immigration Museum opened to visitors. More than two million people tour Ellis Island each year. In the museum, visitors can explore more than thirty different galleries filled with artifacts, displays, maps, and historic photographs. Other features include recordings of oral histories and ethnic music, two theaters, and an immigration library. Tourists can explore the place where so many immigrants—perhaps even the visitors' own ancestors—passed. All help to tell the story of Ellis Island.

Glossary

detain: To hold back, usually for observation. Many people were detained at Ellis Island while waiting for information that would allow them to enter the United States.

favus: A highly contagious, fungal skin disease.

goiter: A swelling caused by a thyroid problem in the neck area.

immigrant: A person who comes to a foreign country to live.

manifest: A list of passengers on a ship.

mark: A unit of German money.

Ottoman Empire: An empire that controlled much of modern-day Turkey, Romania, Greece, Ukraine, Israel, Syria, Iraq, Iran, and many other countries. Although the Ottoman Empire had lost a great deal of territory by the middle of the 1800s, it did not collapse until after World War I (1918).

quarantine: The act of keeping a diseased person away from healthy people so that the illness will not spread. Quarantine also refers to the area where the sick people are kept.

Pronunciation Guide

Frédéric-Auguste Bartholdi	FRAY-day-reek oh-GOOST bahr-TOHL-dee
Rafael Guastavino	RAHF-ay-ehl gwah-STAH-vee-noh

Further Reading

Lawlor, Veronica. *I Was Dreaming to Come to America: Memories from the Ellis Island Oral History Project.* New York: Viking Children's Books, 1995.

Levin, Ellen. *If Your Name Was Changed at Ellis Island.* New York: Scholastic Trade, 1994.

Quoin, Patricia Ryon. *Ellis Island, A True Book.* Chicago: Children's Press, 1998.

Stein, Richard Conrad. *Ellis Island.* Chicago: Children's Press, 1994.

Watson, Mary. *The Butterfly Seeds.* New York: Tambourine, 1995.

Touring Information:

Ellis Island Immigration Museum is open from 9:30 A.M. to 5:00 P.M. every day of the year except December 25. Extended hours are in effect in the summer and during holiday periods. The island is only accessible by ferry, which visitors can take from Battery Park in New York City or from Liberty State Park in New Jersey. For more information about visiting Ellis Island,

write to:
Statue of Liberty National Monument & Ellis Island
Liberty Island
New York, NY 10004

or call:
(212) 363-3200

or visit the website at: <http://www.ellisisland.org>

Index

About the Author

Robert Young, a prolific author of children's books, created the *How It Was* series to enable readers to tour famous landmarks through the experiences of people who did or who may have lived, worked, or visited there. Robert, who makes his home in Eugene, Oregon, teaches elementary school as well as visits schools around the country to talk with students about writing and curiosity. Among his other literary credits are *Money* and *Game Day*, titles published by Carolrhoda Books, Inc.

Acknowledgments

For quoted material: p. 5, David M. Brownstone, Irene M. Franck, and Douglass L. Brownstone, *Island of Hope, Island of Tears* (New York: Rawson/Wade Publishers, 1979); p. 13, Brownstone, *Island*; p. 23, Brownstone, *Island*; p. 32, Peter M. Coan, *Ellis Island Interviews: In Their Own Words* (New York: Facts on File, 1997); p. 39, Brownstone, *Island*; p. 47, Brownstone, *Island*; p. 55, Coan, *Ellis*.

For photos and artwork: © Roger Tully/Tony Stone Images, p. 1; © A & L Sinibaldi/Tony Stone Images, p. 4; Brown Brothers, pp. 8, 18, 20, 27, 36, 37, 53; Corbis-Bettmann, pp. 9, 38; © Grace Davies, pp. 12, 28; Rare Books and Manuscripts Division, New York Public Library, Astor, Lenox & Tilden Foundations. From "Album des Travaux de Construction de la Statue Colassale de la Liberte Destinee au Port du New York", Paris, 1883, p. 14; © Catherine Gehm, pp. 16, 22, 29, 43, 44; Corbis/Bettmann-UPI, pp. 19, 30, 51, 54; Culver Pictures, pp. 26, 35, 45, 46; Lewis W. Hine Collection. United States History, Local History and Genealogy Division. The New York Public Library, Astor, Lenox and Tilden Foundations, p. 52; Klaus A. Schnitzer, pp. 56, 57 (left); © Robert Maass/Corbis, p. 57 (right); Harry J. Lerner, p. 58; © Jon Riley/Tony Stone Images, p. 59; © Phil Degginger/Tony Stone Images, p. 60.

All maps and artwork by Bryan Liedahl. Front cover: Klaus A. Schnitzer.